# MIGHTY Casey

By **JAMES PRELLER**

Illustrated by **MATTHEW CORDELL**

FEIWEL AND FRIENDS

New York

A FEIWEL AND FRIENDS BOOK
An Imprint of Macmillan

MIGHTY CASEY. Text copyright © 2009 by James Preller. Illustrations copyright © 2009 by Matthew Cordell. All rights reserved. Printed in Singapore. For information, address Feiwel and Friends, 175 Fifth Avenue, New York, N.Y. 10010.

Library of Congress Cataloging-in-Publication Data Available

ISBN-13: 978-0-312-36764-0
ISBN-10: 0-312-36764-3

Book design by Rich Deas
The art was created in pen and ink and watercolor.
The text was typeset in 16-point Agfa Rotis Semisans.
Feiwel and Friends logo designed by Filomena Tuosto

First Edition: March 2009

10 9 8 7 6 5 4 3 2 1

www.feiwelandfriends.com

With respect to the original "mighty Casey"
as imagined by Ernest Thayer,
this book is dedicated to Casey Stengel's 1962 New York Mets,
and lovable losers everywhere.
Bases loaded, two outs, I'm rootin' for ya. — J. P.

For Aunt Wanda — M. C.

The outlook wasn't brilliant
for the Delmar Dogs that day.
All summer long, the Dogs
lost every game they played.

Yes, it's true, the Dogs had guts,
and the Dogs had heart;
but catching the baseball, well,
that was the hardest part.

Still, the hounds took the field
with bounding, bursting pride;
win or lose, they did their best;
they could always say, "We tried."

For the loyal moms and dads,
the games were not easily enjoyed;
it was tough to watch their eager pups
so mercilessly destroyed.

On a team that was truly
awful, one player stood out—
little Casey Jenkins was
the worst by far, no doubt.

It's unkind to speak ill
of a batter who can't hit.
So, um, gee . . . that Casey . . .
he sure could chew and spit!

Casey's every at-bat ended
not with a bang, but a whiff.
Yet Coach Lapinski noted,
"At least the breeze was stiff!"

| INNING | 1 | 2 | 3 | 4 | 5 | 6 | 7 | 8 | 9 | R | H | E |
|--------|---|---|---|---|---|---|---|---|---|---|---|---|
| DOGS | 0 | | | | | | | | | | | |
| LIONS | 5 | | | | | | | | | | | |

One day, the game began poorly
and went from bad to worst;
the lowly Dogs were quickly down
five-nothing in the first.

Omar scraped a knee;

grape juice spilled
on Lapinski's shoe;

Ronald the runt had to pee,
and figured left field would do.

Ashanti fell fast asleep;

Tommy Maney climbed a tree;

the team looked badly beat.
Jamal got stung by a bee!

Sally Sanchez tripped and fell;

Johnny Reel refused to run;

but Casey boldly proclaimed:
"The game is not yet done!"

Bloopers, flubs, drops, and blunders—
the Dogs could do nothing right.
Still Casey declared, "We won't
surrender without a fight!"

When Jinn Lee clubbed a homer,
the fans stood and cheered.
The Dogs scored at last.
Said Lee, "That's, like, sooo weird."

Larry Briskie, feeling frisky, took a pitch high and outside.

He swung hard at the next one and gave that ball a ride.

Hit by hit, and base by base,
the Dogs rallied and sparked.
"Strange, we might actually win,"
a stunned Lapinski remarked.

In the final frame, the Dogs
needed three runs to tie.
Alas, O'Malley whiffed, and
Reel hit a harmless pop fly.

When Omar ripped a shot to left
the stands almost exploded.
Sanchez singled, and Bloomberg, too!
Two outs, the bases were loaded!

A fan yelled: "The bases are juiced!"
"Who is on deck?" one wondered.
"Oh no, it's Casey Jenkins," he groaned.
"Coach Lapinski blundered!"

TAP — TAP

Casey strode to the plate
and gave his cleats a tap.

He shut his eyes,
swung with might . . .
and laced a rope
into the gap!

Omar cruised home easily.
Sanchez, she did the same!
Bloomberg rounded third and scored—the
Dogs had tied the game!

Casey's cleats kept chewing soil . . .
the catcher stretched for the ball . . .

Mighty Casey dove for home . . .
and awaited the umpire's call.

Oh, somewhere in this favored land
a crowd is surely singing.

A ball is flying somewhere,
and bats are surely swinging.

For the Dogs, the day is done.
The end has come, but not the same.
Yes! Shout it loud, cheer wildly:
The Dogs just won a game!